THUNDER AND CLUCK

W9-CYG-089

The **Brave** **Friend** Leads the Way!

For Bennett & Lawson
—J. E.

With Love for My Old Man,
who gave me the Sea.
Thank you, Dad.
—M. T.

SIMON SPOTLIGHT
An imprint of Simon & Schuster Children's Publishing Division
1230 Avenue of the Americas, New York, New York 10020
This Simon Spotlight edition August 2021
Text copyright © 2021 by Jill Esbaum
Illustrations copyright © 2021 by Christopher M. Thompson
All rights reserved, including the right of reproduction in whole or in part in any form.
SIMON SPOTLIGHT, READY-TO-READ, and colophon are registered trademarks
of Simon & Schuster, Inc. For information about special discounts for bulk
purchases, please contact Simon & Schuster Special Sales at 1-866-506-1949 or
business@simonandschuster.com.
Manufactured in the United States of America 0721 LAK
10 9 8 7 6 5 4 3 2 1
Library of Congress Cataloging-in-Publication Data
Names: Esbaum, Jill, author. | Thompson, Miles (Illustrator), illustrator. | Title: The brave
friend leads the way! / by Jill Esbaum; illustrated by Miles Thompson. | Description: Simon
Spotlight edition. | New York: Simon Spotlight, 2021. | Series: Thunder and Cluck; #2
| Summary: On a hot day, two unlikely dinosaur friends find a dark, cool cave, but who
is brave enough to lead the way in? | Identifiers: LCCN 2021003369 (print) | LCCN
2021003370 (ebook) | ISBN 9781534486553 (hardcover) | ISBN 9781534486546
(paperback) | ISBN 9781534486560 (ebook) | Subjects: LCSH: Graphic novels. | CYAC:
Graphic novels. | Dinosaurs—Fiction. | Courage—Fiction. | Friendship—Fiction. | Humorous
stories. | Classification: LCC PZ7.7.E78 Br 2021 (print) | LCC PZ7.7.E78 (ebook) | DDC
741.5/973—dc23 | LC record available at https://lccn.loc.gov/2021003369 | LC ebook
record available at https://lccn.loc.gov/2021003370

THUNDER AND CLUCK

The **Brave** **Friend** Leads the Way!

Written by **JILL ESBAUM**

Illustrated by **MILES THOMPSON**

Ready-to-Read *GRAPHICS*

Simon Spotlight

New York London Toronto Sydney New Delhi

HOW TO READ THIS BOOK

THUNDER and CLUCK are here to give you some tips on reading this book.